AND WE SHALL SHARE THE SKY

Written by Alli

Illustrated by Brady

ISBN 978-0-9986124-8-5

Published by Seed Star Books, an imprint of Pleiades Press

University of Central Missouri

Cover art by Brady Stoehr
Book design by Sarah Nguyen

First printing by Seed Star Books, an imprint of Pleiades Press, 2017

Financial assistance for this project has been provided by Missouri Arts Council and the University of Central Missouri.

And We Shall Share the Sky

Written By
Allina Robie

Illustrations By
Brady Stoehr

A long time ago, before the world that you now know, the day was ruled by a vast blue sky and the dark of night was only interrupted by the distant glittering stars, each winking in turn. This was before Sun and Moon dawned into the sky, when they lived instead together as brother and sister on the Earth.

Across the world and throughout cultures, people knew them by different names – Mawu and Gleti, Helios and Selene, Sol and Luna – but everyone knew a story of how they came to share their light with all of us.

Despite being as different as two could possibly be, Sun and Moon loved each other with all the light in the world. Sun brought the energy of the day everywhere he went. And Moon carried with her a calm that can only be found in the stillness of night. Nestled at the base of a mountain range, sat the cabin they shared for as long as anyone could remember.

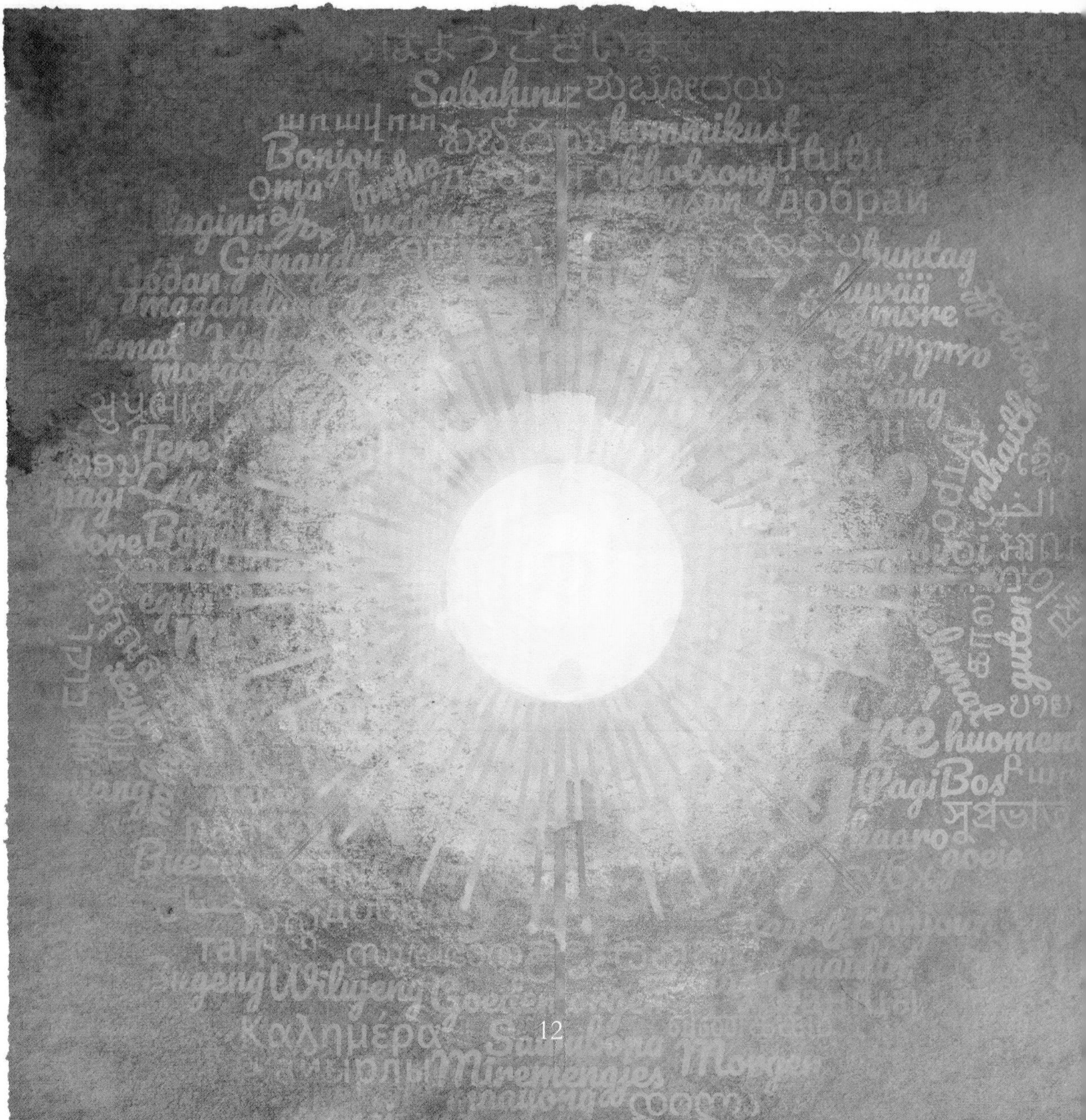
Sabahiniz
Bonjour
добрай
Tere
Καλημέρα

Every day Sun would say, "GOOD MORNING, Moon!" with such shine and radiance.

And every night Moon would give a glowing smile to her brother and say, "Goodnight, Sun."

Sun spent his days exploring every nook in the ridges of the mountains and his light was useful in the caves. He always believed there would be something new to find and was always coming up with some new quest to undertake with his friends.

Moon admired her brother's enthusiasm for adventure, but found her own joys among the changing colors of the pine, aspen, and cottonwood trees. The river was her favorite place to have a paintbrush in hand.

As the wind would wiggle its way through the trees, she captured the leaves in their dancing act. As the squirrels were on the move, she blended in the colors of their food-filled cheeks. Moon took the beautiful, active world and let it rest in her art.

"Moon, won't you come with us on our hike today?" asked Doe, who always took it upon herself to keep everyone safe and out of trouble.

"Not today, I had this dream and I'm just itching to draw it out."

Just then Fox, the quickest creature in all the range, came sliding through the front door, nearly knocking the stack of canvases out of Moon's arms.

"Sorry! My bad! So, are we ready? The top of the world awaits! I hear they call it Elbert."

"Top of the world?" asked Moon.

"Well, one of these peaks has to be the tallest!" said Sun as he strode in with confidence.

"Just don't fall off! I don't know what I'd do without my other half." Moon said. She was setting off on a short walk to the river, humming to the song of the trees as she went. She couldn't wait to paint that dream.

Sun wandered and climbed and climbed some more, determined to find something of wonder before he went home to Moon. He was at it all day. Doe turned back to visit her sister, Fox got bored and ran in a new direction, but Sun kept going up the mountain.

He had been climbing for so long, that there was now no doubt in his mind that this was indeed the highest mountain in all the range.

Meanwhile, Moon made great progress on her painting. With each stroke of the small brush, a contrasting scene of light and darkness came to life. Lost in the work and her own pulling thoughts, Moon was startled when someone started speaking to her.

"I know this story. But it was by water in the way I heard it. They went by water." River was an old friend of Moon's, a silent supporter. Flowing with life, she made for a peaceful companion. But they never spoke much, just enjoyed the presence of one another.

"How do you know? I haven't even finished yet."

"I have arms in many parts of this world and in each place I have a friend, like you are my friend here. I have seen this story before."

River shifted her current towards the painting. "All a little different, but all with the same fate. Your work is lovely, my dear."

With one last exhausted step, Sun finally summited the mountain. As he leaned over to catch his breath, "What...?" With only the goal of reaching the top in mind, Sun hadn't taken the time to notice the scene around him. He moved his feet through the white fluffs on the ground, "Clouds?" he asked no one. But then...

"No, no, no! It's SNOW!"

"Snow? Wait, who said that?"

"Me, Elbert! The tallest peak in all the range!"

"Elbert. Wow. I — I — I'm Sun." He lifted his head, but all words or thoughts got lost, lost in the view. From Mount Elbert, Sun could see the world and the world could see Sun. His brilliance was like a beacon, and all the animals down the mountainside and across the valley lifted their heads to see the light coming from the tallest peak. In his light, the green of the trees and blue of the sky found their meeting place with the white snow-capped mountains.

"This is incredible!" Sun said. "You can see everything! The range must go on forever. Moon, would love this!"

35

Awestruck, Sun stood with his toes in the snow and his eyes on the range for several long minutes. Then he asked, "What is it like up here, Elbert? What do you do all day?"

"Well, I think and imagine. Sometimes I like to create tales about what is going on down in the valley or what those other peaks are up to. Sometimes I imagine horses racing across the sky with a golden chariot in one direction and white bulls pulling a silver chariot in the other. Other times, I call over a storm and play with the snow."

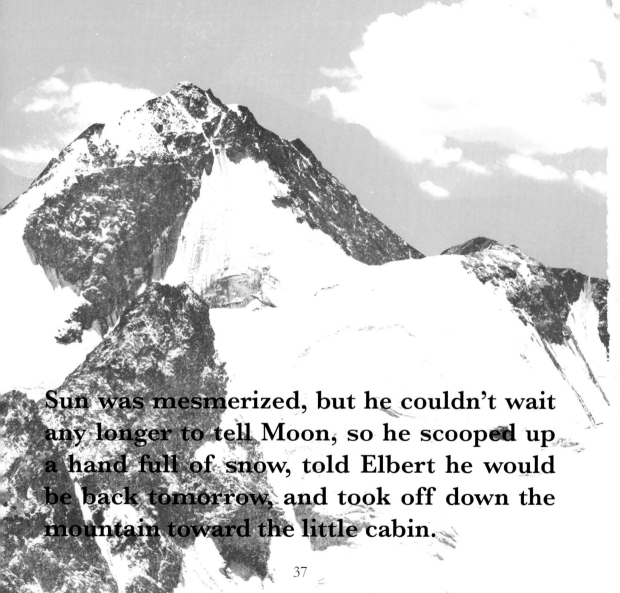

Sun was mesmerized, but he couldn't wait any longer to tell Moon, so he scooped up a hand full of snow, told Elbert he would be back tomorrow, and took off down the mountain toward the little cabin.

Sun came bursting through the door. "Moon! You won't believe — Moon?"

She wasn't there. He peaked in each of the small rooms and couldn't find her anywhere.

"Of course! She must still be at the river!" So he flashed out of the house and over the hill to the river. Moon was there with paintbrush in hand. "Moon—" Sun stopped when he caught a glance at what she was painting. It was like a dream he couldn't quite remember. "Is that—?"

"Oh Sun, I didn't hear you come up! How was the top of the world?"

Whatever Sun thought he saw on the painting snapped away as all the excitement rushed back again.

"Moon! Yes! I made it to the top of the world and his name is Elbert! He told me about the storms and the snow! Look! I brought some back for you!"

But when he opened his hands, they were empty. "But I had some right here."

"What was it?" asked Moon.

"Snow! It was snow, Moon! Elbert can make the storms bring him snow! He likes to imagine like you, but he still plays for hours like me! You need to see it, Moon" and with that Sun finally took a breath and melted into the hillside so that he could gaze up at Elbert.

Moon gave a small smile to Sun and looked up at the tall peak too. She was going to show Sun the painting from her dream, but for now she packed it up with the rest of her supplies instead.

For a week, Sun spent every day at the summit. On Saturday, Moon was surprised when she came up from the river to find Sun in the cabin, and even more surprised to see the mess around him.

A few boxes lay across their small living space, most were empty. Moon noticed her book collection had been stacked in the corner, and Sun's hiking gear looked have been sorted into piles.

"Sun? What are you doing?"

"Packing! I've decided it is time we move, we've been living in this cabin forever and it's time for a change."

Fox came banging around the corner with a box in his arms, "Did you know you had so many art supplies in the back room? There's enough paint here to color half the range!"

Doe emerged from the back room with another box that rattled with Sun's rock collection. "You want to carry these rocks all the way up the mountain?"

"Wait, wait. The mountain? Sun, what is going on here?!" Moon was not one to get very upset, but, at this, she could feel herself getting warmer. "You weren't going to talk to me first?"

"No."

"Well, what if I don't want to go?"

At this, Sun paused. Sun and Moon had never been separated and had never wanted to be. "Why wouldn't you want to go?"

Moon looked closely into Sun's eyes. She wondered if she should tell him her dream, but –

"I'm ready for a break. What's for lunch?" Fox interrupted.

Moving up the tallest mountain in all the range was about as difficult as it sounds, but through every trip Sun was bright and radiant.

"You might not like the idea now, Moon, but I promise when you see these views –" Sun's eyes glazed over for only moment as he pictured the colors again. "You just have to see it."

Moon had never been able to stay angry at anyone, especially Sun. So pushing her doubts aside, she picked up a book and put it in a box.

Moon made her first step up to the summit with much less confidence than Sun had, but in a matter of seconds all of her doubt faded and she was starstruck. She had always known that the world was a work of art, but the waves of color brought tears to her round silver eyes.

She exhaled "Oh," but it was all she could manage at the time.

As a welcome gift from Elbert, snow started lightly falling, slowly accumulating around their feet. Sun beamed brighter than ever and his light worked its way through the range in a way that convinced Moon. She knew she had to tell Sun about her dream and show him her painting.

"Sun, I've been meaning to talk to you about… well, I've had this dream for quite some time and have done this painting about it and I think it's time that I share it with you." Moon turned the painting around to face Sun. Several moments passed, but Sun kept his eyes on the painting, soaking in every line and stroke.

"But Moon, I don't understand. We've been together forever."

"And we would still be together, Sun. Just differently. You said it yourself that it was time for a change and I have been feeling that way for some time. I love the summit, but I think we are meant to go even higher."

The snow flurries began to grow thicker and heavier; Moon reached out her hand and caught several large flakes right on her palm. Fox and Doe were rolling in the drifts and their laughter echoed over all the trees and down the valley.

But as the snow continued to accumulate, deeper and faster. The wind began to blow. "Something is wrong." Elbert said.

"What do you mean?" asked Moon.

"The storm. It should have blown out by now, but it is only getting stronger."

Both Sun and Moon looked around. Elbert was right, everything was covered and the snow had risen several feet in just a few minutes and it continued to fall.

Sun and Moon were both scrambling to stay on top of it, but as soon as they did, another few feet fell and they had to keep climbing up.

"I think this is it, Sun – this is what I saw in my dream," Moon said, as she reached for her brother's hand.

"I don't want to leave you, Moon – you're my best friend!"

"We won't really be apart, Sun. This is right, this is what we are meant for."

Sun knew that Moon was right. They held onto each other for a long time. And then they let go.

"I love you, Moon," Sun called as he slipped into the vast blue sky and found his place among the perfect white clouds.

"I love you, Sun" Moon smiled, as she turned and made her leap in the opposite direction. She was welcomed by each and every star.

"We will share the sky" she thought to herself, just like her dream.

About This Book

Most cultures have a story of how the sun and moon came to share the sky – Sol and Mani, Selena and Helios, Mawu and Gleti. Inspired in part by these stories and in part by Donna Lathem's award-winning play, And We Shall Share the Sky, Allina Robie has retold and adapted the story to a setting in the Colorado mountains of her childhood.

Committed to inspiring young people at all stages of their education, each year SeedStar Books publishes an adaptation of a play that was performed for young audiences on the University of Central Missouri campus by students in the Department of Theater and Dance. The authors and illustrators of these titles are also UCM students.

About the Creators

Allina Robie graduated from University of Central Missouri with a B.A. in English and minors in Creative Writing and Marketing. While she has a perpetual case of wanderlust, and is currently living abroad, Allina always leaves a piece of her heart with her two beautiful nieces, Alexis and Penelope, to whom she dedicates this book.

Brady Stoehr is an illustrator living in Kansas City, Missouri. He received his B.F.A. from the University of Central Missouri and is a life-long student and teacher. His artwork has appeared in numerous books, publications, and galleries. He is a multiple recipient of the Mid-Missouri emerging artist award, the John Lynch Memorial Scholarship in Illustration, and a McNair Scholar.

Donna Latham's plays have been produced coast to coast and around the world. And We Will Share the Sky was a Kennedy Center Regional Finalist for the David Mark Cohen Playwriting Award and recipient of the National Theatre for Young Audiences Playwriting Award from the University of Central Missouri.